No Place for a Pig

Story *by* **Phyllis Root** *and* **Carol A. Marron**

Illustrations by **Nathan Y. Jarvis**

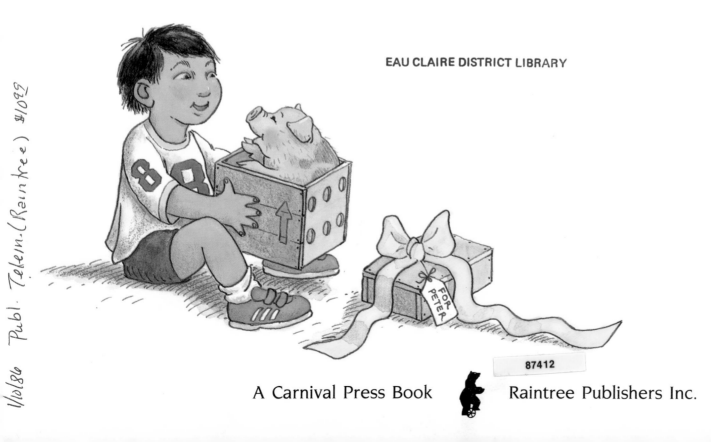

A Carnival Press Book   Raintree Publishers Inc.

Published by Raintree Publishers Inc.,
Plaza East Office Center, 330 East Kilbourn Avenue, Suite 200, Milwaukee, Wisconsin 53202.

Art Direction: Su Lund

Printed in the United States of America   1 2 3 4 5 6 7 8 9 0 89 88 87 86 85

Library of Congress Cataloging in Publication Data
Root, Phyllis   No place for a pig.   "A Carnival Press book."
Summary: After his pet pig Cynthia creates havoc in the house, Peter decides to find her another place to live.   1. Children's stories, American. [1. Pigs—Fiction. 2. Pets—Fiction] I. Marron, Carol A. II. Jarvis, Nathan Y., ill. III. Title.
PZ7.N6784No   1985   [E]   84-17729   ISBN 0-940742-46-2

No Place for a Pig

For Jim, with love.
— P. R.

For Angela and David.
— C. M.

For Michi.
— N. J.

The day that Cynthia gobbled the garbage,

toppled the bookshelf,

and broke down the bed, Peter's mother said,
"This house is no place for a pig!"

So Peter scrubbed Cynthia, packed her favorite pillow,

and set out to find her another place to live.

Peter liked Mrs. Mallory's garden.

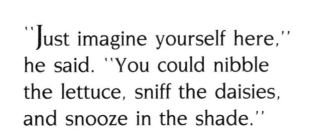

"Just imagine yourself here,"
he said. "You could nibble
the lettuce, sniff the daisies,
and snooze in the shade."

But the daisies made Cynthia's snout itch. She could only imagine herself wheezing and sneezing and snuffling through the garden.

So she tugged Peter down the street.

"How about the nursery school?" he asked.

"I can picture you wallowing
in the sandbox, rolling in the
grass, and playing tag with
the children."

15

Cynthia peeked in at the window.
The children were decorating piñatas.
She could picture herself being painted
and pasted and hogtied . . .

. . . and she dragged Peter along the street.

Peter thought the diner might work.
"Can you see yourself here?" he asked.

"You could gnaw the steak bones,
munch the parsley scraps, and
chomp on the potato peels."

But the cook was making ham and beans, and the diners looked hungry. Cynthia could see herself being roasted and toasted and served on a platter . . .

. . . and she hauled Peter away.

Peter thought the gas station was too smelly.
Cynthia thought the bowling alley was too noisy.

And both of them knew
the butcher shop would never do.
The only place left was the woods.

"I don't know," said Peter.
"Do you think you could be happy here?

"You could nestle in the toadstools,
root in the swamp,
and search for friends in the gloom . . . ."

Just then something rustled in the woods,
something hissed in the woods,
something howled in the woods . . .

. . . and they both raced all the way home.

"Mom, I'm back," hollered Peter.

"I looked everywhere, but I couldn't
find another home for Cynthia."

Peter's mother gave them both a hug.
''Come outside,'' she said. ''Cynthia's
grown too big for this house. But she
still belongs here with us.''

"Cynthia knew that all along," said Peter.
"And so did I." He helped his mother nail
on the last shingles. Together they tucked
Cynthia and her pillow inside her new house.

VERBS are words that express action or state of being. Every sentence must have a verb. Action verbs such as **shuffled**, **leapt** and **ran** are an important part of strong writing.

Did you notice other action verbs in this book? Notice how these words from the story express an action: **gnaw**, **munch**, **chomp**, or **tugged**, **dragged** and **hauled.** Can you find other examples in the story?

Verbs — just one of the many ways you can have fun with words.

Phyllis Root lives in Minneapolis, Minnesota, with her husband and daughter. She has written several books. *Gretchen's Grandma*, which she co-authored with Carol Marron, received a 1983 CBC-NCSS citation as a Notable Children's Trade Book in the Field of Social Studies.

Carol A. Marron lives with her husband and three children in Minneapolis, Minnesota. She is also the author of *Mother Told Me So*, a CBC-IRA Children's Choice Book for 1983.

Nathan Y. Jarvis is an illustrator and fine artist who has made his home in faraway places, from Munich, West Germany, and Salzburg, Austria, to Pasadena, California, where he graduated with honors from Art Center College of Design. Mr. Jarvis, his wife Michaela, and their children, Jakob and Maria, currently live in Kansas City, Missouri.